TO . . . .

FROM . . . .

RABBIT GETS READY

For Tom and George and
with thanks to Evie

A Red Fox Book

Published by Random House Children's Books
20 Vauxhall Bridge Road, London SW1V 2SA

A division of Random HXouse UK Ltd
London Melbourne Sydney Auckland
Johannesburg and agencies throughout the world

Copyright © Claire Fletcher 1995

1 3 5 7 9 10 8 6 4 2

First published in Great Britain by The Bodley Head Children's Books 1995

Red Fox edition 1999

Printed in Singapore

RANDOM HOUSE UK Limited Reg. No. 954009

ISBN 0 09 187291 X

RABBIT
GETS READY

Claire Fletcher

RED FOX

RABBIT woke up feeling different. Today was a very special day – his first day at a new school. He was excited and happy, but he was nervous too and there was a strange feeling in his tummy. It was eight o'clock. He had to get dressed quickly if he was going to be there on time. He didn't want to walk in late with everyone looking at him – Rabbit felt quite weak at the thought.

He opened his wardrobe. He had lots of clothes; coats and trousers and shoes, and shirts and jumpers. What should he put on? 'Everybody else will know what to wear,' thought Rabbit. It was so unfair.

He tried on his knitted swimming costume.
It was great for diving and somersaulting at
the pool, but not quite right for school.

Next Rabbit put on a striped jacket and a straw hat. He had spent a lovely day with Dog on the river bank eating peanut butter sandwiches and looking at the boats. Maybe… The jacket was smart enough, but the others were sure to laugh at him if he wore *that* hat.

What about his beloved dungarees, with safety pins where
buttons should have been. He usually wore them chug-chugging
along on board the big red tractor at the farm. But Rabbit threw
them on the floor. Everyone would think he was a real scruff in
those.

Rabbit's funny feeling was growing. All he wanted was to fit in.
It was such an important day, but he just couldn't seem to make
up his mind.

He unruffled his best hat, trimmed with feathers. It had been such a hit at Monkey's party. But no, thought Rabbit. He didn't want to draw *quite* that much attention to himself. Not on his first day anyway.

Rabbit frantically rummaged about. Something big and bright caught his eye. It was the jumper aunt Maud had given him last summer. 'I expect I shall be quite warm enough without *that!*' said Rabbit, scornfully.

Rabbit glanced at his watch. 'Oh dear, Oh dear, I'll be late if I don't find something soon,' he sighed.

He spotted his blue sailor suit and tried it on. As he marched up and down with a nautical air he could almost taste the salt and hear the call of the seagulls. Rabbit was beginning to wish that *he* could run away to sea. As far as he knew, sailors didn't go to school.

Poor Rabbit. Suddenly he heard the beep beep of the school bus
outside the door. There was no time to lose. Rabbit grabbed the
last thing from his cupboard – his stripy football jersey. He ran
out of the door as fast as he could, clutching his lunch box in
his paws.

The schoolyard brimmed with all the colours of the rainbow. A group of pigs and cats were having a picnic in the middle. There was a water trough with boats and ships and there was even a tortoise on a big red tractor. Rabbit wanted to join in, but the funny feeling in his tummy was worse.

He felt very alone and just a little bit scared.
Then he saw a small bear standing timidly in the corner of the playground. He did look smart, but he didn't look very happy. Rabbit took a deep breath, marched over and took the bear by the paw. 'Are you new?' said Rabbit. The bear nodded, shyly. Rabbit smiled. 'Come on then,' he said.

Together they ran as fast as they could to the end of the playground. 'Kick it here…' 'To me…' came the cries from all around. Rabbit jumped for joy – he would soon make friends. And his funny feeling had quite, quite gone. Perhaps tomorrow he would wear… 'Oh bother,' thought Rabbit. 'Who cares…' And he let out a shout – 'Let's PLAY!'

THE END